from an idea by Andrea Dami

Illustrations by: Marco Campanella
Text by: Anna Casalis
Design by: Stefania Pavin

ISBN 1-84135-375-2

This edition first published 2005 by Award Publications Limited,
27 Longford Street, London NW1 3DZ

Printed in China

Billy Brownmouse
Won't Eat His Dinner!

English text by Jackie Andrews
Illustrated by Marco Campanella

AWARD PUBLICATIONS LIMITED

Billy Brownmouse gazed out of his bedroom window. "Just look at all that snow, Stilton!" he said. "Aren't you glad we're inside in the warm? It must be ever so cold out there."

Stilton was Billy's teddy bear. He didn't say very much.

"Billy!" called Mama Brownmouse. "Run and wash your paws now. Dinner's ready!"

Billy!

Mama put Billy into his special chair and helped to tie his bib. Then she tied a little bib on Stilton.

But Billy Brownmouse suddenly decided he wasn't hungry.

"Bleh! Carrot soup. I don't want it!" he said. "I want to go and watch the snow." And he folded his arms, turned up his nose and refused to eat even a mouthful.

Now, Billy!

Mama Brownmouse sighed. "Come on, Billy. Carrot soup is your favourite. Try just a spoonful. I made it specially for you, with new baby carrots."

"Well, I don't like carrots any more. They're a funny colour. And I don't like soup either!"

Mama's whiskers began to twitch, as they always did when she was running out of patience.

"Would you like some lovely, fresh, creamy cheese instead?" she asked.

"No, I don't like cheese any more, either," said Billy, firmly. "I just want some sweets."

And he got down from his chair, picked up Stilton, and stomped back to his room.

Mama Brownmouse was very cross. Her whiskers quivered and her foot tapped on the floor furiously.

"There will be no sweets until you've eaten your dinner, Billy!" she told him. "You won't grow big and strong on sweets! Be thankful you have a lovely hot dinner – the poor animals living in the wood in all this snow, can't find enough food to eat!"

Huh!

Now, Mama's words had made Billy Brownmouse think very hard. He had many friends who lived in the wood, and he began to worry about them.

Just then he heard a tapping at the window.

Tap! Tap!

"What's that?" wondered Billy, and he went to look.

"It's m-m-m-me, B-Billy! Charlie C-C-Cricket! Please let me come in!"

Charlie was frozen. "I'm so very c-c-cold," he said. "Could you spare me a little hot soup, or some cheese?"

Mama Brownmouse frowned. "Oh, Charlie. Every winter it's the same. You never put enough food away in the summer! All you think about is singing and enjoying yourself. Well, it won't do!"

Although Mama Brownmouse scolded Charlie, she was very kindhearted and would never turn anyone away hungry. "Come on, then, Charlie," she said. "You may as well have the dinner I cooked for Billy. He says he's not hungry and only wants to eat sweets!"

The carrot soup was still piping hot. Charlie Cricket did not need to be asked twice.

"Mmmm! This is delicious!" he said between spoonfuls. "You are a wonderful cook, Mama Brownmouse!"

"Oh, that feels so much better!" said Charlie. "Do you really not want to eat this fantastic soup, Billy? You don't know what it's like to be really hungry. To have nothing else to eat but what you can find in the snow! Soggy pine-cones and frozen bark!"

Now that Charlie was warm and full of food, he felt like singing and dancing again.

As they said goodbye, Billy couldn't help thinking about the things his friend had told him.

"Soggy pine-cones and bark!" he thought. "That's horrible!" Suddenly he felt very hungry. "Is there any dinner left, Mama?" he asked.

Luckily, Mama Brownmouse had made plenty of soup. "Of course, my funny little mouse!" she said with a smile. "And I think there's even a bit of cheese."

Billy Brownmouse licked his soup bowl clean, and then ate every last crumb of cheese. It made his mama very happy to see him enjoy his food.

"Thank you, Mama!" he said, giving her a kiss. "Next time I don't want to eat my dinner, I shall just think of the poor animals in the wood. I won't be naughty again!"